# "Ladies and Gentlemen!"

Written by Dana Meachen Rau
Illustrated by Jim Caputo

*Reading Advisers:*

*Gail Saunders-Smith, Ph.D., Reading Specialist*

*Dr. Linda D. Labbo, Department of Reading Education,
College of Education, The University of Georgia*

## LEVEL C

# A COMPASS POINT
# EARLY READER

*For Charlie, a great entertainer*

## A Note to Parents

As you share this book with your child, you are showing your new reader
what reading looks like and sounds like. You can read to your child
anywhere—in a special area in your home, at the library, on the bus, or in
the car. Your child will associate reading with the pleasure of being with you.

This book will introduce your young reader to many of the basic
concepts, skills, and vocabulary necessary for successful reading. Talk
through the details in each picture before you read. Then read the book to
your child. As you read, point to each word, stopping to talk about what the
words mean and the pictures show. Your child will begin to link the sounds
of the letters with the look of the words that you and he or she read.

After your child is familiar with the story, let him or her read the story
alone. Be careful to let the young reader make mistakes and correct them on
his or her own. Be sure to praise the young reader's abilities. And, above all,
have fun.

Gail Saunders-Smith, Ph.D.
Reading Specialist

Compass Point Books
3722 West 50th Street, #115
Minneapolis, MN 55410

Visit Compass Point Books on the Internet at *www.compasspointbooks.com* or e-mail your
request to *custserv@compasspointbooks.com*

**Library of Congress Cataloging-in-Publication Data**

Rau, Dana Meachen, 1971–
   "Ladies and gentlemen!" / written by Dana Meachen Rau ; illustrated by Jim Caputo.
     p. cm. — (Compass Point early reader)
   Summary: A child is very nervous about the possibility of not remembering what to say in the
play.
   ISBN 0-7565-0120-2 (hardcover : library binding)
   [1. Stage fright—Fiction. 2. Theater—Fiction.] I. Caputo, Jim, ill. II. Title. III. Series.
PZ7.R193975 Lad 2001
[E]—dc21                            2001001596

Everyone is excited

for the play to start.

# My heart is pounding.

My stomach is growling.

My voice is cracking.

My lips are frozen shut.

Now the audience is coming in.

I still can't remember my lines.

My palms are sweating.

My hands are shaking.

My eyes are staring.

My forehead is dripping.

# Now the lights are dimming.

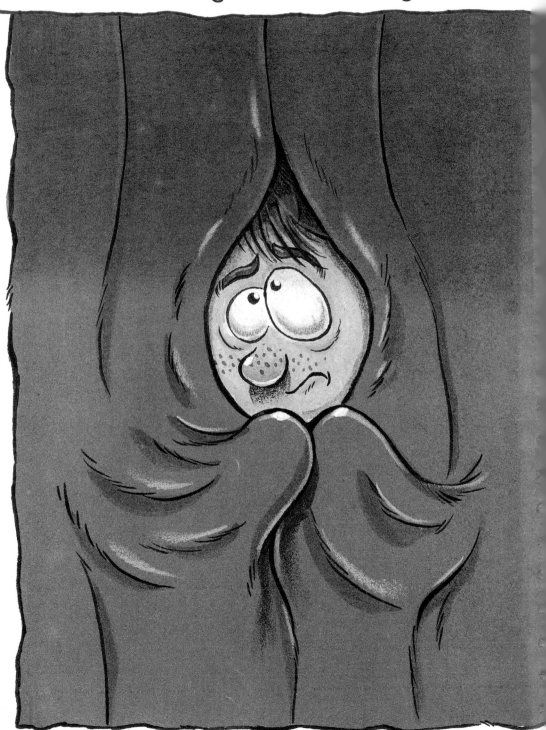

# What am I going to do?

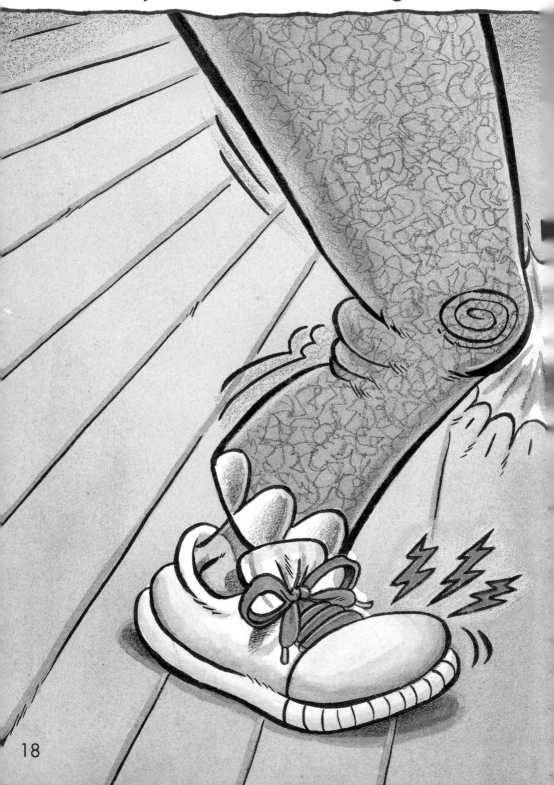

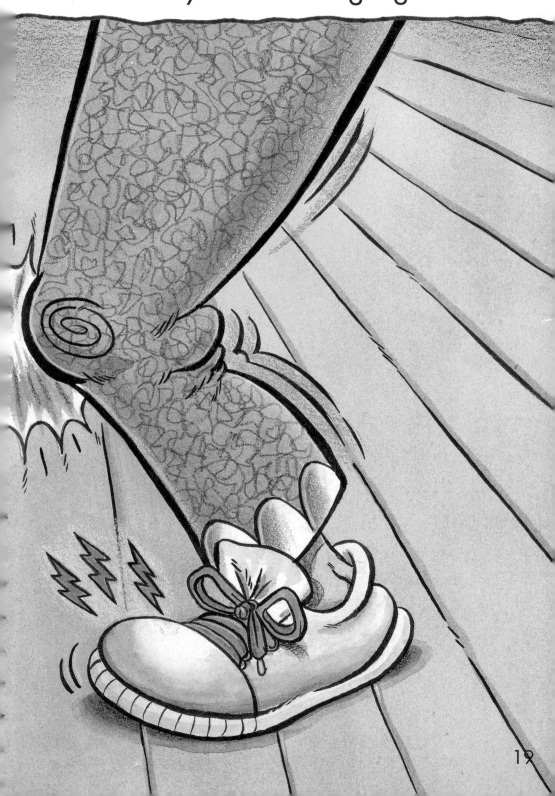

My costume is itchy.

It's hard for me to breathe!

Now the curtain is rising.

I see my mom and dad.

They smile, and I pretend

I'm practicing my lines at home.

"Ladies and gentlemen," I say.

# "Welcome to our play!"

# More Fun with Plays

Performing in front of other people is an ideal way for your child to show off his or her talents, learn the importance of practice, and even overcome shyness. If your child has never been in a play, help him or her put together a play of his or her own.

• Help your child think up characters, a setting, and a simple story.

• Involve your child's brothers and sisters or close friends to play the different parts.

• Collect clothes, paper, or other objects and let your child imagine how they could be used for costumes and props.

• Let your child and other characters act out the story. You don't even need to worry about a script. See what creativity sprouts from their own ideas.

• Encourage them to practice, practice, practice!

• Invite family or friends to be the audience.

• If your child feels nervous, remind him or her that whatever they do, they have done a great job. Bravo!

# Word List

(In this book: 71 words)

| | | |
|---|---|---|
| am | hard | pretend |
| and | heart | remember |
| are | home | rising |
| at | I | say |
| audience | I'm | see |
| breathe | in | shaking |
| can't | is | shut |
| coming | it's | smile |
| costume | itchy | staring |
| cracking | knees | start |
| curtain | knocking | still |
| dad | ladies | stomach |
| dimming | lights | sweating |
| do | lines | the |
| dripping | lips | they |
| everyone | me | tingling |
| excited | mom | to |
| eyes | my | toes |
| for | not | voice |
| forehead | now | what |
| frozen | our | welcome |
| gentlemen | palms | |
| going | play | |
| growling | pounding | |
| hands | practicing | |

### About the Author
When Dana Meachen Rau was in third grade, she was in her first school play. She played the role of Patti Peanut. She only had one line, but she was *very* nervous. That's why she never became an actress. Today, Dana writes stories and draws pictures in her home office in Farmington, Connecticut. She still gets nervous if she has to talk in front of a lot of people.

### About the Illustrator
When he was an eight-year-old Boy Scout, Jim Caputo had to sing a song in front of all the moms and dads. But when he opened his mouth, nothing came out. He tried again and still nothing. That's when Jim decided that drawing for people was much easier than trying to sing for them. When Jim is not singing in his car, he is drawing and painting at his studio in Orlando, Florida.